CONTENTS **Page**

I WANT TO TALK TO YOU

I want to talk to you –
and curse the time I
wasted -
I want to hold you close –
not your body
but your tired soul –

I want to wander with
you and explore the essence of
the grass –

Pause with you and be startled
by the movement of a silent
snail –

I want to share with you
unhurried, un-monied things
and learn the few painful
messages I do not already know

I want to be spiritually alone
with you and play freely from
dawn to dusk –
Among lazy things –

Bending now and then
to pick daisies and mossy
musk –

I want to travel with
you to silent places –
Where our footsteps
would be so soft
that no lark would stir
or cloud move in the
heavens –

I want to weep with
you and tell you of
dislikes and needs – without
burdening you – you
understand –

I have a need of you –
not physical – but
my soul is flying
out there in search of
yours – If such souls
are allowed to travel
heaven-wards or out of
worldly things.

ANNIVERSARY POEM

"Give me, something personal"
he said,
I smiled sadly to myself,
Because for twelve years he
has had me,

Twelve years I have
lain in the shelter of
his love and affection,

And if my voice lacks the
same warm inflection,
as his,
It is the way life has taught
me to be.

When young, younger than nine,
I gave love to everyone –
And reached out for the
same warmth,
As a new lamb on thin
legs, gambols in the sun.

But where I stepped there
were shadows, and my
hands grew cold;
Still I tried, until one
day –
When young, I grew old,
And no longer looked for
the sun –

But ran rather to the shadows,
and walked with the rain
in the meadows –
I grew as the poplar tree,
Tall, cold, with shimmering
tresses –
But even poplar trees give
love and shelter to the birds –
Which leaves them free –
So it is the same with me.

And you my dear are my
roots –
Without your warmth – they'd
wither and die.

So don't sigh for "something
personal" from me –
For if from time to time I
bend and whine –

Shiver and shout, don't loosen
the clay of my bed –
But give me my head –
And allow me – my birds –
Which are my poems –

This one is yours, and also mine,
Because a tree is forever
bound by its roots –
So will we be –
Until nature says
And sets us both free.

First published in *Woman*

SELF ACCUSATION

As a Poet – I am eloquent –
As a Woman – I am proficient –
As a Mother – I am indulgent –
So why does my heart still
shout –
    As a *human being* you
    are not sufficient.

I FEEL

I feel like a woman,
stripped of her jewels
robbed of her pride –
Left on the outside on a snow-
white Christmas Eve;
With 6/2d – not enough to
buy a meal – a bed –
But too much to spend
on a cup of tea –

I feel like the beggar,
stripped of the riches of his
trees and honeysuckle lanes,
his valleys, and dark green
secret places, where he finds
shelter and warmth –
Sleeping in cold clean sheets and
heavy blankets –

I feel like a one-legged
woman – watching her husband
dance,
While her dead limb twitches
to the music

I feel like a perfect lawn
plagued by mole hills, – a
ripe cornfield forcing itself
to stand upright in spite of
heavy rain

I feel like a woman
with one child –
Who has suddenly grown
from babyhood to maiden-hood
    Oh! God
    I feel like a WOMAN

HUE – AND THE CRY

(To my daughter Tracy)

The houses she draws,
Are so gaily painted –
Windows red, orange and white

Her sky is blue – bright and light,
Her meadow is –
The greenest I've seen –

Her garden well it's orange too –
But it matches the windows –
And as the years blow
Heavy knowledge into her mind,
She'll paint it green –

And only dream of the days
When she could paint a garden
Orange – a sky pea green – and
a house crimson and blue.

I think the colours
are lovely – and the hue –
– Well it goes with the
mind
        Unspoiled and true –

I wish I wrote my
Poems –
        Bright Pink Blue.

THE MASSACRE

Today I watched silent –
My breath stilled to a
gentle hush –

Then as if in a tremendous
rush
Spring grew –

And my eyes were aware
That I was being stared
at
By a crescent of crocuses
Yellow, bright white and some
With an almost indescribable blue –

Large, bossy colourful heads,
on such thin delicate stems,
They strained – white veined –
To hold upright their bold load –

Their task should have lasted
longer –
Until the delicate stems grew
stronger –
And the wind warmer and
not cold and blustery as now

But how they tried, this
colourful throng,

Until – the still was broken –
by the voices of clustering children
Who ran shoe shod into them
and over –

Today I wept silent –
And prayed that the daffodil
would prove more strident –

I looked at the crushed dead
bed –
And was sure the veins in the
white stems were red –
        Blood Red.

ELYSIAN

Hurry! dance, swirl, curl,

But do it, do it now,
For time is short –

And you, delicate snowflake,
Have only as long as it takes
To reach the ground –

Not for you, the moulding,

Folding your lacy shapes,
Into hideous human
effigies
You, and your white companions,
Seem to know,
That for the fragile, fine
Wind washed snow –

There is no soft cushioned bed,
With others of your kind,
Nothing – but the swirling,
curling rush –

The melting –
And the Silent Hush.

AUREVOIR LES TEMPS HEUREUX

The thing we shared was as
intangible as the web of a
young spider – struggling with
its first thread,

We shared the secrets of the
timid breeze,
As a starving sparrow gives
a crumb of bread
to its hungry young,

When heaven sent us rain
the sting was but a caress,
Tantalising like taffetta
swishing softly under a
heavy dress –

You and I shared so many
delicate things,
Like untidy toadstool rings,
We listened joyfully when the
wind blew blustery messages
to us,
and compared it to the
swishing of fly-ridden tiger tails

Do you remember when –
feet dangling in ditch water –
We would hitch up our clothes,
and watch dragonflies – twitch – doze

Then fly zig-zagging with long –
blue translucent tail lagging behind

Can you recall – the first leaf
to fall?
And the excited rush – the
breathless hush, when it was
caught in eager hands?

Yes we shared such intangible
things – you and I,
and if sometimes my heart,
head, spirit, or whatever –
cries –
We know you can't come back –
        Don't we?
                You and I.

DAISY CHAINS

Yesterday was warm, and I
wove daisy chains in dreams
I threaded them.

Yesterday was the nape of a baby's
neck, soft and damp
I nestled in it.

Yesterday was the coal fire
glowing ready to flame
I sat close to it.

Yesterday was unreal in its
total reality –

Joy in the belief that you knew –
I wove dreams around
our spirits.

Today is the future, and the present
I must face –

Yesterday is the past, and
I'll not venture there again.

Except to weave my daisy chains,
While holding my baby
Close to the fire.

COMPARE ME TO THE GREEN-FLY

I am the green-fly grub –
tended in the dark – milked
dry of my emotions.
Then left out in the sun –
abandoned, to dry.

Compare me to the insecure
green-fly.
Clinging close to the diseased rosebud –
destroying the strong clematis –
Too afraid to let go and try my delicate
wings –

So I stay here among others
of my kind, tending the grubs,
ignoring the wind –
stirring in my wings.

Until stronger arms bear the grubs away –
Down into the dark warm ground –
Where the only sound is the strong
being fed –
In exchange for giving the grub a bed.

So compare me to the green-fly
and its grub –

Perhaps the wind will be kind –
and blow hard –
forcing me to fly – or I'll just sit here
eating my rosebud –
and watching the clematis die.

WOULD WE KNOW?

How can you pin-point, pigeon-hole
the intangible?
Corner the West Wind
When it is barely warm?

How can you tell the exact moment,
When the reeds begin to whisper,
or when the placid cow – still in the
field, momentarily ceases to chew –
The minute a mushroom takes
form and is born in soft,
brown earth?

I ask you all these things,
Not from a desire to know –
But rather to show you that
such is the closeness of the
intangibles of music poetry and art –
If we had met in the corner
        of a warm mushroomed
field, caressed by the reeds' whispers,
and stared at by the large sympathetic
eyes of a cow –
would we, all of us joined in
        that precious elsinore time
Know?

AMINOSSOS – CRETE 1973

Minds can go only
as far as the souls
reach
ZENITH

can teach

No astral lessons
to ease
Man's pain –

Minds are prisoners of
the body
Acceptance total –
being the only Parody.

ALL

The mighty feeling of being
alone –
The sense of total atonement –
for being human –
and
Being woman – vulnerable!

The feeling of unity between
the
Elements around – until
All is fused into one
Mighty Force and
To last – like the scented vapours
as they drift – enfold
you –
and
Take you back from whence you came.

TO A RUNNING TODDLER SEEN IN GLADSTONE TERRACE

Don't run past the puddles,
Jump in every one –

Don't worry about dropped
ribbons –
Free hair is much more fun –

Don't wash your jam-kissed lips,
Jam tastes so much better than soap –

In fact, wet, scruffy, rain-soaked little
mite,
Change nothing, on you it looks
all right.

WIMPY BOY

The grubby face reflected in the
mirror
showed no emotion

That was none other than
jealousy, hunger and a
haunting longing

Jealousy being a negative emotion
longing for the colourful knicker-
bocker glory

The silver spooned boy
sucked back
noisily savouring every
colourful mouthful

The other, busily fingered the
red-wrapped sugar cubes
pocketing a few
and disdainfully shifting his
eyes belying
hunger, wishful lust and the
lack of money
wishing being a negative emotion

It seemed as if the long
glass had no bottom
and was like the cruse of oil

never to be completely empty
though others may have hoped so
it was finished and the gulf of
money was bridged between them

Cuts, grazes, scrapes were
once again
first priority
he would forget the twitching and curling
of the dry tongue
and the imagination
clinging to the parched throat
of cool cool ice cream.

Only when he grows up
will he remember the times when
he couldn't afford a knicker-bocker glory
life will teach him that
lust, jealousy may be negative emotions
but oh, my dear innocent boy
you will explore oceans
of wishful thinking.

WOMAN/AGES

I'll live again through
you
child,

Problems will become
nothing
but
rainbow flying fish

I'll live again through
you
child

Remembering each
forgotten wish

as I watch
those

rainbow flying fish

I'll live again through
you child
and
remember my
mild winters
and feel cold –

Watching through
my woman/ages

The wild warm
life in you
          my child

SHE IS HOME

She is home,
with soup-spoons
tinkling
bell-like, and

She sits, like
a crinoline lady
bell-like, and

She has rain/wet
hair swinging
bell-like, and

She chatters with
the excitement of
a stream of
jingle bells –
child-like,

She glows with
the tender
discovery of
youth,

She sees every
blue-bell's bell
bell like –

She is home,
home and the
home is a church
pealing with laughter
          bell-like.

I AM THE VESSEL

I am the vessel into
which you
pour yourself.
I am empty.

I am the empty shell
awaiting a snail
I am nothing.

I am the angel hovering
on the brink of hell
I am despairing.

I am last year's
nest.
I am waiting.

I am the poet born
awaiting
        re-birth.

Bear with me.

LESSON

Lessons must be learned,
as new leaves in
chapters of relationships
are turned –

Lessons of how to speak
gently without the
bruising quality of
love – turning
twisting the words
into opposites –

Lessons must be
learned, the heart
must learn to be
still, when racing
like a startled
goldfish in a
bowl
much too small,

Lessons of not touching,
when every sinew aches to
touch, and the whole
of one's being longs
to enfold the one
being that teaches you the lessons

of missing,
waiting, and
one learns – without
being told
the most heartbreaking
lessons of all,
be still, don't touch
or you would have
        to be told.

ALL THE LOVE IN THE WORLD

All the love in the
world
could be held in
the cup
of the hands which
so casually
captured the look.
All the words in the
universe
could be written in
the paper-thin
book.

IT WAS THE PURPLE TINGE ON THE ELDERFLOWER

It was the purple tinge
on the
elderflower –
Multiple purple heads –
that reminded me
of her

It was the way
the candle blew
that made them
appear as little children
dying on the Cross.

It was the gentle wind
that blew paper off real roses
that
blew the scent of her.

It was the gentle way
the tree let go of
its fruit –
And although
purple
stained
No crown
No uncertainties
Only Love
lay bound.

THE INVITED VOYER

I have a vague discomfort
in my mind –
of something I felt, something I
saw.
I have a palm/sweat fear
of seeing this again –

This lip/kiss this non hugginess –
This very – adultress –
Gives a vague discomfort
in my mind.

Not being a voyer I was
placed in that
foul smelling place –
Where purity is lost and
children become adults –
Made by adults to be
children –
Then force fed with "Growmore"
to be adults.

Drinking wine like one
who loves the bottle
more than these silent
lip/kiss situations –
I knew if I counted to 10 –

Then one green eyed girl
was going to fall.

BLOOD TESTS

Sensitive to the feelings of Christians
she knows her place – and flick fingers
Her golden cross deep between her
clothes – aware as she does of
a feeling of deep insensitivity to
herself.

She waits her turn, looking at
"warnings" about health avoiding
those that are shaped like hearts
with main arterial roads –
So much like those she wished
she had travelled.
"Outer road leads to life"
"Inner road leads to where she sits
waiting to hear – what her weary
travellers have to tell her –

Sensitive to the feelings in her fingers
she longs to take up the golden
cross and hold it close in her palm –
But nothing gives her the smile
reserved to those "in the know".

She wonders what the "In Crowd" would do
if she stage whispered
"I'm sure Jesus wants me for a sunbeam"
I've been called so often –
Being sensitive to the feelings of
others she keeps quiet and waits.

"Room 2 please" –
and stripped she waits –
Hypocrite?
Sunbeam? – or just an
insensitive Christian?

SHE IS DOING HER NAILS

She's doing her nails
when worlds erupt –
Massive decisions are made
Icebergs are thawing and
travelling to the Thames –
She's doing her nails
each studied brush stroke
erases such happenings

She chooses colours carefully –
Yellow for the smog travelling
over Sumatra –
Purple for the punk/gothic
return.
She sits patiently
doing her nails –
Her mother told all
who called at doors or telephoned.

Be Quiet, NO terrible noise/like news –

She's doing her nails.

I HAD WATCHED HIS WEB GROW

I had watched his web grow
you know –
And in the growing felt his
pride –
All symmetry the whole world
hung in his making
and dazzling shone the sun
on his dew dropped jewels.

I'd watched him daily
feeling my strength match
his and wishing
but only in part –
to be the anchor to his
shimmering ship of
dead fools.

The breeze wafted
his cargo of flies
and insects from
strange worlds
he didn't inhabit.

He wove them all
into his web and
then his being.

Today I heard
laughter from my bed –
and the chorus of
"He is dead, he's dead, he's dead"
splintered the dreams
of his making.

Sadly I marked the last
thread of his making and
little by little I carried
on rebuilding – praying
one leg, one eye, one sight,
of my alter-ego
might survive.

I TASTED THE SOURNESS

I tasted the sourness
of the elderberry
before its sweetness
fell between us.

I was bruised and my
being crushed by
the carelessness of
random feet –
Moving, moving, moving
as only bruised elderberries
can – I folded into
soil/pavement cracks
to avoid the peck, peck, peck
of the
greedy/seed searching
splatter beaks.

I wondered where the others
went – those that were
left hanging on boney branches.
I wondered, I wondered if
they unlike my kind
had a second chance
a second flowering –
that would allow them another
fruiting a second glint in
the dying summer sun.

I had to keep moving, moving
so I crawled up and
was crushed into a
basket of others of my
kind –
The world was mine and I
was wine spinning, spinning.
I had tasted sweetness
It was enough.

AN OLD MAN CLOSED A DOOR

An old man closed a
door to a lifetime's memories
With his suit buttoned and
Sunday shirt on – waited
looking at the clear open
sky – and closed the door.

Hiding behind a paper –
pretending not to hear
the final gentle shutting
of the door – didn't help.
It wasn't raining but the
paper had holes through
which eye rain penetrated.

I belong to a place where
people say change is good
and old photographs just memories.
I belong to a place where
young rabbits never grow
up – never taste the
first flower head or
lie waiting for the
gun to shed its heavy load.

I belong to a place where
dreams come true and
sun-sitting and talking of
nothing that mattered –
happens all the time.

No messages splashed
into storm orphans or
did anything more important
than slip backwards up
a rainbow –
I mentioned time? – Did I
dare to mention time? Time?
Well all these happenings
go on all the time - but this time

An old man closed a
door to a lifetime's
memories
With his suit buttoned and
Sunday shirt on – waited
looking at the clear open
sky – and if I
failed to mention it
before –
Let his tears fall
into the rain butt
and closed the door.

I remember he
had told me he
couldn't bare
waste –

SOMETHING CHILDISH BUT VERY NATURAL

Just like that,
and its over.
Gone are the days
when my being
rested, in crested paper,
gone are the bitter
every day frays,
in which
my soul
was never tested
Being and Soul just
rested, rested
and rested.
Not now, the painful
ecstasy
is back
in
my breast.
Emotions extreme
are being put
to the
test,
although well trained
in the articulate
pain,
I've never ridden
on this particular train
and I fear

that the
carriage
will not
hold the frame.

I'm leaving, I'm leaving,
on the painfilled
train
"something childish but very natural"
tells me,
I won't be coming
back again.

DYLAN THOMAS
ST. MARTIN'S GRAVEYARD

Such a bold bright
beauty
she was
Who stopped her golden
head
upon
Dylan's dark green
clad bed.

Such a silent chime
did echo
LOUD
louder than the
Six Bells of Laugharne

From within her
crinoline yellow
folds –

Such a wondrous
sight, she was
stooped there

CLOSE – CLOSER than
the living ever were
to the
Dylan she loved
        in death.

SOMETIMES

Sometimes I've seen a grubby net
curtain – move,
I've seen the arthritic thongs
move clumsily –
Like children with toast – on too
hot prongs.

Sometimes I've seen a face,
White, topped with wispy hair,
But when caught looking, she stopped
the game – I was declared unfair,
Like children, peeping through
fingers, when others run and hide

Sometimes my heart silently cries,
I feel for you, I ache almost love you.
Then the faded eyes meet mine,
And I halt my youthful whine
Because the old eyes, see beyond me
to far off days and skies with
        an un-aeroplaned blue –
Those eyes say – 'I pity you'

TO ROBERT GRAVES

The sun behind
the Mountains
Grows cold –

The Caesar behind
in his Palace –
Looks old

The princess with
no name
has died.

GRAVES

Moved like a dark shadow
Old poet with moonstone
eyes,
framed by a silver ring.
I watched you as a dog
waits for the rustle of
its lead –
waiting for the biting
truth – the wisdom –
wanting the precious gift
of word/life
trembling I sat at
your feet,
Old poet with moonstone
eyes –
moved like a dark shadow
past me and
muttered
'Wife'.

ONE MORE TIME

I'll walk over the bowling
green one more time,
Dig my heels in the
cricket pitch one more
time –

Stand by the busy roadside
and cry
not heeding the passing
crowds or traffic
passing by –

Pounding my fist against
telephone box windows
One more time

When tired from my walk
exhausted and bleeding from
my grief –

I'll settle wise and still
sitting like a dead dove
on the sill of lost life
and utter sounds
that may remind people
Vaguely
        of
          a
            Dove

FOLLOWING HARDY

Rooks cluster together
in the frowning
black sky,
like words thrown
together without
thought from the
ledge
of man's tongue.

Black cattle herds
muse moodily at
blackened winter – bare
branches.
A LARK FLIES HIGH!

Monstrous electric scare-crows
steel arms spread-eagled
order all off except the
non-caring
black headed gulls.

'The Madding Crowd'
ghost it over Hardy's
country and today
old William Barnes,
buckle-shoed and
speaking music to
his dead wife –
revisits –

holding her ghostly body
pressed hard against his
black cloak –
convinced for eternity
that Tennyson's
'diety' was his only hope.

Lonely souls dwell
in the dark museum
corners of Dorchester
and even
Bed & Breakfast signs
BLACK.

WE TALK ABOUT THE WEATHER

Stripes, greys, browns
just a dash of colour,
Broken handbags, discarded
mother/dreams
A room once filled with hope.

Old Vogue mirrors and
modern Snoopy/verses
replace black and red polkadot
Bunny –

'Do you dance the Polka?'
'Do you dance the Polka?'

Half filled cups of tea
with rimmed stagnant
a glass of water stands
abandoned –

'Tea for two – and me for you'
'Tea for two – and me for you'

Fading Grandma
photo settles into the
dust and no sign
of mother here –

Mother did *you* hear
no sign of mother here –

'People who need people
Are the luckiest people
in the world' –

Children visit for a
while, offer wet kisses
damp curls at nape
of neck and at
Twenty – check out
move out –

Mother and Father sit

'Like Sister & Brother'
'We talk about the weather'.

SENNEN COVE - AUGUST 1971

The sea opened wide, white jaws –
And laughed until –
The white foam –
became as light as settled beer
froth.
He chewed on his meal –
and then, well fed –
Threw up the lifeless carcass
to the dribbling, irritated
sand.

Dunes stuck out like
bloated cow sides – and
moved – as if
half afraid of the over confident
jubilant sea –
Like a woman, used to being
wooed
Finding her man arrogant –
With his gentle boyhood – long forgotten –

The sea, like a whipped savage
dog,
Withdrew almost slyly back into
itself –
leaving only spray covered cars –
perched high on the cliff top,
To sit silent – watching the
dead carcass –

Moved restlessly back and forth –
By the fitful, half frightened sand –
To whom the gulls wheeled and screamed
        JUDAS   JUDAS   JUDAS

A POEM

Not asking anything
because to become
a
Wanting Person
Demands some speech.

BLACK CURRANT STAIN II

If the Black Currant stain
still shadows my cheek –
I'll paint white powder
in deep strokes
until I
become as a clown

If the nose glows
with the reflected shine
of rivers of tears –
I'll rub it red as a
cherry
to match my powder-white
face –

If the mouth refuses to
smile, because of the anguish
of missing you –
I'll draw big smile-lines
So no-one will know –

Oh!
and
if I can't eat and grow
too thin
I'll sew on big cushions
of comfort
all over my pain-racked body

To go with the

White Powder
Red Nose
Big Grin
                    and
Being
Too thin –

and no-one will know –
that as seasons go
I weep with the snowdrops while
my face turns to ice –
I hide in the sunflower shade when the heat
beats me down

I shuffle neck high in
leaves in the Autumn and colour
myself with their hues –

Oh! and
when Christmas comes
Why it's no problem
at all –

I'll stand at your window
all fat and rotund –
with White all over
my face –
and coal black eyes
and grinning mouth

While drinking your wine
and laughing –
you'll see
something staining
the pure white statue
of snow –
standing so still behind
your Christmas Tree
feel a cold shudder
and turn away fast.

Because you won't want to see
the Black Currant
stain –

Crudely covering me.

THE WAY OUT

The
Way Out
is not through the
madnesses
of
Love
THAT is the
way in

The path to
illuminative
Love
is the one
through framed
pictures
which depict
the languages
of the
Blesséd

So
sliding
between glass
and frame

I sit in
a
tea-cup
full of
buttercups –
picking
strawberries
with new-born
lambs
playing at my
feet
and love clouds
tumbling around
my neck

The Way In
was not
sign posted
and so
in love
am I
with illusion
that to
try to find
the 'Way Out'
would be
Delusionary.

I'VE MISSED MICHAEL

I've missed Michael in
Doncaster, Leeds and Matlock –
But never on a Tube –

I've missed Michael at
parties, picnics and long walks
But never on a plane –

I've missed Michael talking
to him – preparing to leave –
watching him plucking invisible
feathers off my bird-like
sleeve –

I've missed Michael while
holding him tight without
touching him at all

I've been the sun commanding
him to shine, the stars
causing him to sparkle

I'll spend my time
missing Michael
watching him grow
miserable, uncertain and
slow –

I miss Michael but
unless he reads this
he'll never know!!

TIME-LESS

Time is of
no significance
to the
self-satisfied
or the self opinionated –
Time is something
to be gobbled up
like food – fast
indigestible –
TIME –

Swallows people,
places, dog walkers
and talkers – who
talk of nothing
in particular
to use up
TIME
passes slowly for those who have
to sift it, sieve
it – to ache
for five minutes
to survive for
10, and recount
the loneliness of
life times takes at
least another five –

TIME to add it
all up – and if the
answer cannot be
divided by two
then it shall be
minus
one

ELIZA (Neé Duncan)

Don't sink back
into pillows
of memory –
letting your
luminous eyes
bye pass me
again –

Too often have
I sought
your gaze
from
running child
in knee
high buttercups
to swimming girl
with tadpole
movements

Don't move your
hand –
black branched
with veins
inside the
sheeted white
of your shell –

leaving me
once more
reaching for
a hand to
hold –

Mother of mine
who fears death's
call –
lift memory from
these grim walls
and hot sticky blankets –
run again with
the long legged girl
and the boy
at your side –
Skim them like
pebbles over
the shimmering
Lodden water –
where warmth
was breeze
tempered –
and
dragon flies
feared none –

Take me back
once more
to pick
diamonds shimmering
with water
from the stream
which has no
end

Stand smiling
at the meadow's
edge as I run
neck high
in corn and blood
red poppies –

Mother of mine –
sinking into your
white cushioned
pillows
Swirl the boy
round once more –
and hold the girl
aloft –
Dancing,
   laughing,
      living,
   in the River Lodden.

I REMEMBER

I remember –
I picked Blue-bells
and 'she' threw
them away –

I remember the sticky stalks
clinging
to my moist excited palms –
She threw them away –

I remember running bare-legged
through whisker grass
legs hot
with nettles –
palms moist and wet from
the crying sweat
of the Blue-bells

I ran
rabbit-fast hopping
over mole-hills
headlong through
the
moist fronds of fern
stopping
dropping
hopping onwards with

my
loving blue burden
not picked
you understand
PULLED
from the very essence of
the earth
and with each long green and
white ended
stalk –

My love poured
giving them warmth –
expelling the
heady sweet perfume
of each curling bell
Why then?
No warning sound
with so many Bells –
Why no whisper
from nature
no scream of pain
as I pulled
each
bell
from her lover's bed

There was NO warning

Later –
red-wheels –
jostling for space
on scalding
legs
and arms moist
palms wet
with tears

A thousand bells
screamed
Blue-bell like –
from the rotting
hell
where she threw
them

Tears Tears Tears
        fell

You shouldn't have
picked them
        She yelled!!!

TONIGHT

Rain sheaths night branches
and
Shumack trees stand stark as
Monarchs of the Glen,
Listening as I do to the
Fox bark –
Minding back to "Clare" his
"cry in the night" –
Tonight there are too many
cries –
the dark roars and
black branches reach to
the ink sky for help

Tonight seated in the
black chair staring
at the sleet and
weeping naked branches
I pressed my fingers
star-fish splayed
flat on the window pane –
feeling that by such
tremendous force
The weeping branches
would cease their endless
waving
and turn and touch my
frozen palms through
the glass –

By such an instinct
I felt nature's pain
and mine –
would be wrapped
lover-like for Eternity.

NOT QUITE NOT EVER (Miss Catt)

She's the egg that
never hatched
The mistress of snow
never virginal
The rose blighted
before bloom

She's the choir without
the descant
The sinner with no
enjoyable sin
Not one to be spoken
about, talked of –
She's a 'miserable' sinner –

"Maud" in a glass case
staring at the garden
and watching those
who walk in it –

It's *her* garden but
they walk in it

It's her glass cage and
they *put* her in it –

She cries more often
now, but not real tears –

they form pools and others
wash and cleanse themselves
in them –

Her tears are the terminal
kind – the ones which
cause eyes to stare
and never blink –

Her tears are the
'hurting' kind

She waits in her glass
cage –
Not deaf not dumb –
But achingly
                    Blind –

TWO WITH YOU

You see it has something to
do
with not looking at you –
feeling you looking at me –

Oh! and it has something
to do
with needing you – and
succeeding with you being
a total disaster –

It has something to do
with tall summer Cow Parsley
and legs swishing, melting
through it –

Oh! and it has something
to do with
Seeing you swirling ahead
in the white heat – and the
shimmering mist –

It has something to do
with being at one with
nature and its universes
and never being at
two with you

I'VE STOPPED MISSING YOU

I've stopped missing
you
no longer search in
fear of finding
you

I've stopped tears
falling into glistening
pools
no longer grief stained

I watch rain sparkle
shimmer and shine –
on fledgéd rose
and willow leaves –

I've stopped writing
letters, cards and
dropping 'phones –

I soar towards
rainbows, sunsets,
and shimmering dawns –
as an albatross
I pause glinting
slyly at the rising
Phoenix –

Laughing I watch
as she plummets
back into her ashes –

I soar on my
heavy white wings
heading endlessly
towards the darkening clouds –

YOU DIDN'T HAVE TO

You didn't have to
send a message
from the grave
for you had
already received
my grief-stained
note
telling you
                    to
                              R.I.P.

WALKING STEADILY UPWARDS

Walking steadily
upwards through
the dark months
I find myself
lingering by
the wayside –
Happily trailing
my bare feet in
summer's dust –

Rushing breathless
into moving white
cow parsley –
humming as the
bees suckle
honey –

I am in no
hurry to
rush
along this
newly found
path –

being content
with all that
is just
ahead of
me –

I have no desire
left in me
to see
what lies
beyond the
fronds of fern
that
brush
my bare
legs –
and gently
chide
the
butterflies –
for being
too flippant –

Nothing is
more
available
and
nothing
more
is
needed
as I walk
steadily
upwards
through the
dark months
towards the sun which is slowly rising.

8 HOURS

Daffodils last
eight hours
in this the
room
I inhabit
when sick –

Like premature
babies
they come in water
and are given no
milk
no glucose
to keep their fragility
alive –

They smell vaguely
warm and just alive
like damp chicks
newly hatched
forced to stand
too tall –

gawky teenagers
in gymslips
they hold
their young golden
heads high –

but this youth
is too beautiful
too tremulous
to stay –

and like teenagers
at their first
Disco –
they fall one
by one
Daffodils last only
8 hours
        hours
                Hours

SO YOU LEAVE

Not really going anywhere

Because in reality you
have
never been anywhere –

I say "I'll miss you"
speaking words/dry mouthed
so someone who
insists –
he has only been the
13th rail – the hopscotch trail –
the touchstone never touched –

I grieve for girl/lass and
woman
Mostly for the child
who still answers
nature's
whispered calls –
who still drops a
stick on stagnant
water –

and waits anxiously
for it to
sail free on
the other side
of the
bridge –

I weep for the
girl
who motherless stands
gazing at the
empty tin bath
in the meadow

Wishing it to be
womb/warm –
Envying the one
who can pass
shoulder high
parsley and not
ache to be
attached to the
flower/stalk/root –

So you leave
and
the vastness of
life
stretches before
me –
and
I tremble
as a field mouse –
surrounded by
Hovering/Hawks.

M ROUTE

He flung the book
at me holding
visions of
my
dead and dying sisters
Chekhov knew
them well and
Tchaikovsky played
to one or two –

These visions were familiar to me
I inhabited
their background
for we *were* sisters

with test tube fathers –
born from a
sperm collected
from random madmen

The book, a
map of the path
I had been travelling
when the M route
was clearly marked –

"I've never liked my
sisters" I protested
"and don't want
to meet them
on the way"
prefering to stray
and play fey games
unnoticed –

"Read the book"
he commanded
My sisters smiled
up at me
from within
the book
of the
dead/dying and the mad

Laughing they chorused
"You've been on
the M route
all the time
the paths
are all closed
We were just
ahead"

"You've been on the
M route all
the *time*"

Mmm

IT HURTS

When this heart –
visualised you understand –
never seen –
hurts –
It can't be stroked,
patted, or gently
caressed –

It hurts –

When this heart - hurtles
along
its uneven path –
jostling with its
arterial roads and
by-passes –
It thumps into
emotions – *and*
It Hurts –

It mutters to itself –

Must sort this out –
Mustn't let this get out of hand
because hearts are never
handled by the occupier

Heart beats – faster
running a race it
knows it can't win –
stops –
Finds itself bleeding in
someone's hands –

Pumping – Pushing – Bruising

It Hurts.

CRASH-DIET

Before me
you
have
laid
a
table of
bored
poetry –

used to
feasts –
I
must content
myself
with
a
dry
hamburger –
Accustomed to love/
pain –
you sound
like

a
sex-starved
spinster
chasing
a
grease monkey –
Seated at
my
table
waiting
to
be served –
I wore
my best
whore dress
wedding white
jester's hat –

I began
my
meal
and
like a
scavenger
running
out of
luck and food –

started my
meal –

I placed the
dish
back on
the
table –
and
started to
eat
the
menu –
I was

Hungry again.

SHE FELL DOWN

She fell down
He never picked her up

She cried until the tears
became as rivers

He swam in them

She almost drowned

He watched others save her

She learned later to
swim
He thought the water too shallow

She stopped crying and
started to laugh

He looked puzzled

She waits contently
Secure in the knowledge

He will swim by
In a river swollen by
his own tears

She will be fishing
at the time

Won't notice him drown

THE PEONY

I saw the blood/red
petals fall –

In silence –
In silence, so loud
that
the very soul of
the earth shifted
uneasily –

So very painful
was their silent
crash –
From stalk to stem
to glass top table –

They lay pink/red
fluted like a
breeze of deflowered
virgins –
abandoned/ashamed

I watched the blood/red
petals shrivel and
wondered why –

I wept for
all young
deflowered
girls –
whose innocence
falls in silence –

I moved –
and with the
wet tear/filled
tissue
wiped the sperm
filled petals
off the mirrored
reflection of
their shame –
and buried them
deep, deep as I
could into the
moist dark earth –
Praying as I
did –
they would flower
again –
        next year?

BREAKING OF PLATES

In the Breaking of
plates –
In the mixing of colours
and
the mountains of mis/match
Ghosts are laid –

In the breaking of
hearts
In the cuts, that
through water weeps –
wounds are solidified –

In the Breaking of
plates –
Something very indefinite
is done
                Breaking plates
                Breaking plates
                        Breaking
                                Breaking
                                        BRAKE

MEGAN

She climbed over the wall
yesterday –

Solemn faced/quiet spoken –

Sensually undoing her
shoes –
laying them side by side –
like lovers silent on crumpled sheets –

She lay back in the
straw backed chair –
arms above her head – languidly
Watching others watch
her –

She fingered the straw
edged chair –
and hugged her knees –
pressing them up to
her dimpled chin –

Hearing a voice I know
was mine –
I questioned this reflection
this deflection of
all I had become –
and

learning forward
wanting to touch
this self image –
felt her breath
hot on my
unspoken words –

Leaning forward from
what was now a
hayrick no longer a
chair –

She plucked a straw
from my
tousled hair –

leaving her
answer

hanging like a
wind blown rose
on the air –

I'm Megan

I'm Child

LOVE POEM

If light should scorn
my darkness –
setting you free –

If a rainbow should splinter
and shard my being –
leaving you colour/bright

If my custard pie
shall fall, not facewards
leaving just the empty
crust –

Enjoy the custard –
letting the yellow
fall over you gently

as a cape of buttercups
headless in a
Baudelaire dream –

If a scream shall
break your sleep –
let me scream
and you be the dreamer

If all the hurt
in a 10 force
storm in a
teacup
shall spill over –

let it be on
my clumsy arm
Oh
and if I can only
buy two presents
having none
other close –

Then I give you
my absence
divided by two.

THE SMOCKED DRESS

Once again I am
Banished to the
Land of no kisses,
No hugs, no smiles –

No man could hurt
As much as this
Young innocent with
Vagrant's eyes –
Who with cleverness
Knows how to
Collect pain and measure
It as he eats the
Chocolate you carefully
Chose for him.

Once again I am
Shoulder/leaning and
Fist wiping stinging
Rain from eyes
That insist rain comes
From the empty barrel
Behind them –
Vanishing from sight
I hear her footsteps
Quicken and long to
See her return in
Her smocked dress
And ankle socks –

Arm wrapping this
Banished mother who
Still weeps and longs
For the warmth not
Felt in her smocked days –

Knowing those footsteps
Cannot return I turn
To an old brown
Envelope – fold it/bend
It to my needs.

I tell you, all of you
Of how it feels to be banished
From the land of kisses and hugs
Footnote:
I've told you, all of
You - but don't
Reach out arms or
Nod heads saying
"You know how it feels" –
Because it's my feeling
My pain and I don't want
Anyone to share it.

WASP

Wet wingéd wasp
I pray
you miss
each pavement crack
each
curling leaf
or crashing petal –

Oh!
Wet wingéd wasp
No bold death
"Saga" Hum –
Just the painful
body/drag to
death to silence –

Kneeling I courted
yesterday's destiny
and moved a
half eaten plum
watching you
plunge –
Soaking in the
Baudelaire drink
Dream –
There was no scream, no question –

Just the acceptance
of something
ever familiar
ever present
in the soft ripe
flesh of the plum –
No stealing needed –
no hesitant visit –

A mothering
A smothering
of
flesh fruit
and sucking silence.

BEFORE THE ENCORE

She moulded a
snow-drop
until
it reached
back into
the earth –

She melted snow-balls
before shaping
the snow
and skated on ice
that hadn't
frozen –

She sang
before the
thrush had
time to
full throttle
his song.

She won
before the
chips were
down –
and
frowned before
the glad
news was
broken –

She invented
speech
before it was
spoken
She clapped
before the
encore
had begun –
And knew
Punch long
before Judy –

She loved
Adam
long before
Eve
She'll be there
crying before
you grieve.

ADA GOODWIN

I saw Ada Goodwin
in the
High Street today –

ankle socked I
raced to keep up –
wiping the tears
from dry eyes
with the
fringe of her scarf –

Racing wet cheeked
to touch her/to
feel this mispent
love of my
youth –

Corners, Corners, Corners,
turned and
STILL the square peg
turning in its round
hole –

Arm loads of heather/hacked from
memory
bushes –
multi-coloured –
tied in
ribbons/satins
to match
her bobbing bows

Gypsy footed/
fire/flecked
chimney/sooted
water/babied
this Cathy
this tormented
heather torn
creature –
screamed
STOP to shadows
which held
no soul/substance –

Turning this
ghost of the
past –
jumped/landed
square footed
and pulling
chalk from
her teeth
white/gleaming
drew two
lines – two lines
across the
top of my
ankle socks –

Marked as I
was –
I marked
"my time" and knew
it to be over –

She danced
away into
the path of
my self/delusion
danced
danced
danced
while I
marked
my time
my time
my time
until the
ankle socks had
all but disappeared
all but
        disappeared.

THE PLACE

I thought of the
place
today –
realising my pace
had slowed to
a skip-stop –
a bed-hop –
a mind-daze –

I thought of the
heat-haze
today –
realising my soul
hovers over
a Green-Man
pub –
a Dragon-Fly
daze –
a grass clump
that's slowly
closing –

I thought of the
hush a bye
place today –

A big-armed Oak
a flat stone in
a rootsome place

I soul marched
out of this place
to that –
floating with
the thistledown and
crashing to the
ground with
abandoned
bird feathers –

I am in "the" place
today –
and my pace has
reached "The Red Shoe"
stage –
I want to stop awhile
by the
hush-a-bye place –
but the pace is
too fast –

I thought of the
place –
today –
realising my pace
had slowed to
a skip-stop –
a bed-hop –
a mind-daze –

MOON SCREECHING

No words can arm/wrap
a soul/mate
Or lean a comfortable
hip distance away
Invisible/feeling warmth
closing until blended
as one.

No indefinite signals
are given as souls
are not earth bound
and are uneasy about
such sharp contact –

No tears can ease
the bruise that
bounces off the beating
heart and rebounds
against the silent soul.

But I have heard
that on "magic"
nights – black
with similes –
Restless with
Hardy's "Hauntings"
and shocking longings –

They
leave love/locked
and are
seen moon screeching
– and

Gently falling
Becoming part of
the whole as
dawn breaks its magic
and forces all
into place again.

I NO LONGER NEED THE COBWEB DRESS

I no longer need the
cobweb dress – which
has so many gaping holes –
I no longer reach to catch
the glancing fly – they
are too heavy for my gown.

I spin out the days with
thoughts of times that have
flown –
Making the holes in my
gossamer gown –
Letting the breeze tease me
off the window – I looked
back and fading, fading, fading
Wondered if I had even been there at all.

I'VE BECOME A DEAR DIARY CASE

I've become a "Dear Diary"
case –
Needing a place
any place –
to efface my
vacant place to.

I've become best friends
with the amoeba, flattened
Together on the sea/soaked
rock –
I cling passionately to the
seaweed bonetted
Jetty poles
Feeling certain there is
a warmth flowing
through us –
Finding myself left
high on damp shingle
I single out one
rough edged shell
to echo my
sadness to –
I lie comforted
by the sound of
my own words –
Whispering back –
"So that happened
to you too" –

I become the
lodger taking the
place of the
life that called the
shell a home –
I don't write in my
diary now –
But as you
pass wet sand –
You may see my message
"Should you ever need
a place – mine is vacant".

THE 'WRITINGS ON THE WALL'

The 'writing's on the wall'
It's
Written in blood
But no one hears
The
Scream of pain –
The writing's on the wall.

Once when short –
Shorter than
The wall –
I tapered cement
With twigs –
And held each
Bug which fell
Stopping its fall –
Not knowing then
That high above
The writing was
Already on the wall

Now as ivy clings
It's green turning
Yellow tipped –
One more I reach
With red tipped
Fingers –
Probing the cement

Holding the ivy
Desperately clinging
To the wall

Probing and pulling
Tearing the tender/rooted
tentacles.
I find dead wood lice
Flat/backed and
Those that live running
Sideways glancing
At the one who
Tears their home
Away from the
Wall –
Whispering only as
Wood lice can –
"She's the one"
"She's the one"
Who wrote
"The writing's on the wall"
"The writing's on the wall"

A WRETCHER'S CHILD

She looks like
a Wretcher's child –
She stares with
chip/chisel eyes –
Her hair in strands
granite/hard –

She is a Wretcher's
child
No wolf can bend
her to him nor –
naked ape suckle
her –
She suckles at
rose-hips – her lips
are the buds –

She is the Wretcher's
child –
no pram to hold this
one – no harness to
bind her in –

She is the Wretcher's
own –
Later
She'll suckle
rose thorns and

sleep in the
cherry stone –
before running
tree high
home – home –
home –

When she cries it
is the oldest
sigh –
the ancient
cry –
of
        The Wretcher's child

TODAY NOTHING PASSES

Today nothing passes
by without the hummsong – without
Patten's "out-going song"
no hanging spider
catches the last summer fly
no bee is starved of
the last sweetness of the
dying rose –
no apple falls and in the
falling is bruised –
no hand will pick
berries and be thorn/pricked
today all is incoming and
warm and spiders will
breathe up their
webs and allow
flies to catch
the last glimpse
of the summer –
for this is what
Baudelaire meant
when he offered
the cup full –
this is the gift he gave and
from it we will
all drink
and share
the summer's
last
        great song

(with acknowledgements to Brian patten)